This book belongs to:

For Jjajja Kafeero, my ever-smiling Kirabo, and the many stories left to tell.
Nansubuga

A papa, et aux jours de pluie que nous n'avons pas pu partager.
To dad, and all the rainy days we never got to share.
Sandra

First published in the United Kingdom in 2018 by Lantana Publishing Ltd., London.
www.lantanapublishing.com

American edition published in 2018 by Lantana Publishing Ltd., UK.
info@lantanapublishing.com

Text © Nansubuga Nagadya Isdahl 2018
Illustration © Sandra van Doorn 2018

Distributed in the United States and Canada by Lerner Publishing Group, Inc.
241 First Avenue North, Minneapolis, MN 55401 U.S.A.
For reading levels and more information, look for this title at www.lernerbooks.com
Cataloging-in-Publication Data Available.

Printed and bound in Europe.
Original artwork using dry pastels on paper, finished digitally.

ISBN: 978-1-911373-39-1
eBook ISBN: 978-1-911373-42-1

Sing to the Moon

Nansubuga Nagadya Isdahl & Sandra van Doorn

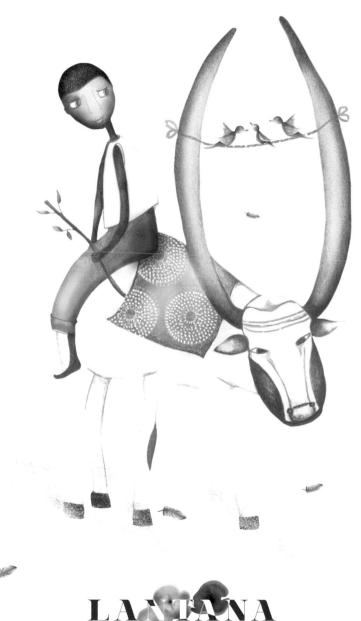

LANTANA
PUBLISHING

If I had one wish, I would reach
the stars, then ride a supernova
straight to Mars!

Jjajja tells me, "Sing to the moon,"
and perhaps my wish will be
granted soon.

With another wish,
I would still go far -
across the ocean
to Zanzibar.

I would sail on a dhow and gaze in wonder at old spice markets

...till the sun goes under.

If I had more wishes I would surely fly!

I would take the crested
crane up high.

After spotting the
forest's mythical beast,
I would land at dusk for
a monstrous feast!

Instead, I awake to the patter of
rain, and watch the clouds spread
like a charcoal stain.

I think of the hours with nothing
to do, except count the drops as
they muddle the view.

But then I
hear steps
on the kitchen
floor, so slowly
I open the
wooden door.

Jjajja is drinking
his hot morning tea
and tells me that he
has been waiting
for me.

As we eat
porridge,
I glare at
the gloom,
announcing
that I'm going
back to my
room!

Jjajja stands tall – and in one, two, three – holds out his hand and says,

"Let's go and see..."

We start in the storeroom to pack away peas, picked when the fields were last humming with bees.

Jjajja remembers
his childhood
best friend

...a boy called
Kirabo whose smile
did not end.

We clear the veranda of wet bamboo leaves

...while Jjajja recalls   climbing up guava trees.

I say I love hiding
in guava trees too

...and he tells me
that's something he
never knew!

The sun slowly sets and
the day splits

...in two.

I help clean tilapia for the fish stew.

Jjajja shares memories of trips as a child, when he and his father would fish in the wild.

With daylight now gone and the dark settled in, Jjajja says our night adventures begin.

He slowly unveils his tall tower of books, where he has stacked stories of bold kings and crooks.

By light of a candle we turn over pages of long ago fables passed down through the ages:

tales of lost cities and
great heaps of gold

...African
kingdoms and
sights to behold.

And then Jjajja leaps to his feet to retell the story of how the sky rose and then fell.

He thrills me with thunderous
bangs! and kabooms!

...then shoos me outside
where the brilliant
night croons.

We hear fires dance and the echo of drums, friends making meals, and the grasshoppers' hum.

And Jjajja reminds me
that I'm always loved

...by even the brightest of
stars up above.

With one last glance at the shining night sky, we bid the sweet sounds of the evening goodbye.

I know then
that even
new worlds
far away

...couldn't compare to this
one rainy day.

And with a tired yawn,
I stumble to bed, where
I am tucked in with a
kiss to my head.

And, like every night,
before leaving the room,
Jjajja says quietly...

"Sing to the moon."

Dear Reader,

Have you ever been stuck at home on a rainy day? What did you do?

Uganda, which is where my story is set, has two rainy seasons: one from March to May and the other from September to December. That's a lot of rain...and a lot of rainy days! This story was inspired by the rainy days I spent with my family in Uganda listening to tales spun by candlelight. My own Jjajja ("Jjajja" is the Luganda word for "grandfather" and "grandmother") was very fond of books and he was the keeper of many, many stories.

In Uganda, like all places, stories can be found everywhere. So, once the rain ends, if you listen closely, the landscape comes alive. With over 300 mammal species, 1,000 bird species (more than half of all bird species in Africa!), and 5,000 plant types, Uganda has remarkable wildlife. The sounds of nature tell unique stories of their own. What sounds do you hear in nature? What stories do they tell?

Well, I hope I was able to take you on a journey with me to Uganda, and I encourage you to listen to the magical sounds and stories around you...wherever you are!

Happy listening,
Nansubuga